GHOULIE

s.z.baucan@gmail.com

ISBN: 978-0692744963 (1983)
ISBN: 0692744967

210
&
200 and 10 books

GHOULIE

written
&
illustrated
by

Scott Baucan

edited

by

Chad Tennant

&

James Howell

I

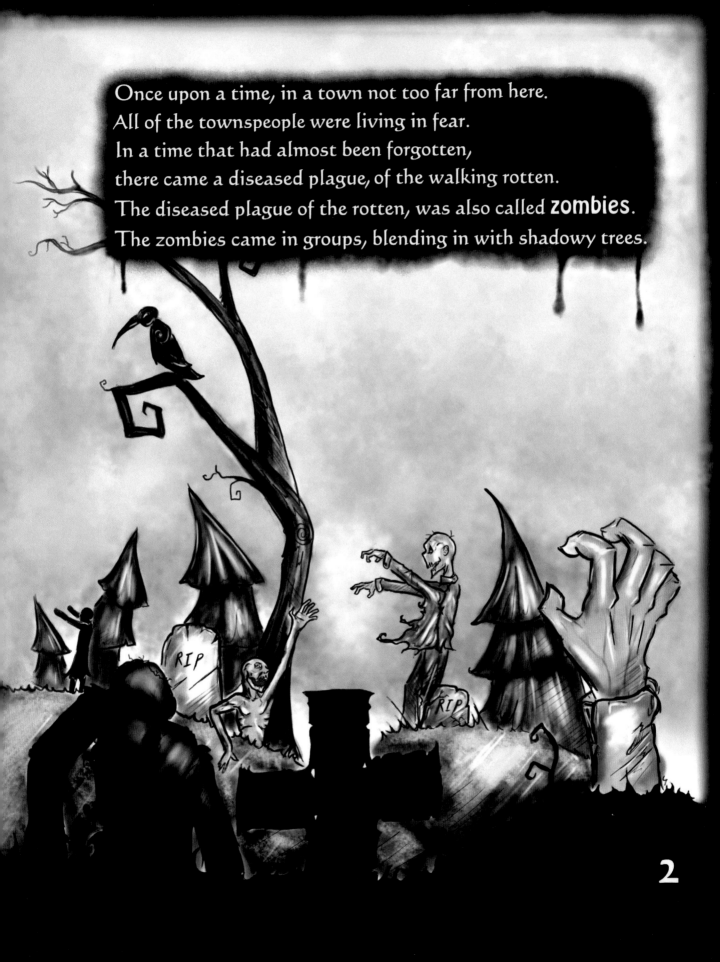

Once upon a time, in a town not too far from here.
All of the townspeople were living in fear.
In a time that had almost been forgotten,
there came a diseased plague, of the walking rotten.
The diseased plague of the rotten, was also called **zombies**.
The zombies came in groups, blending in with shadowy trees.

2

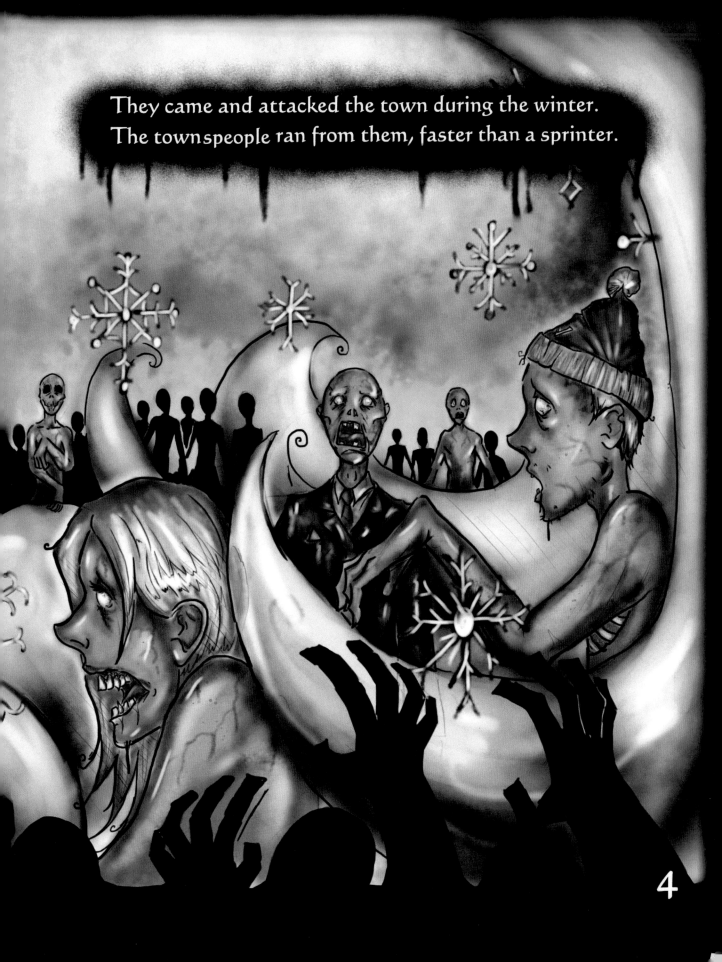

The zombies left, just as fast as they came.
Marching to the next town, with a terrible shame.
They faded away into the distant twilight,
leaving the echoing winds, of winter's coldest night.

All of the zombies left the town, but one.
The truth of this very story, has begun.
Under a nearby streetlight, the snowflakes sparkled and glared.
It stopped a child-like zombie from leaving, as it stared.
His past, we may never know.
His name, gone like melting snow.

At this very moment in time, we will just call him **Ghoulie**.
Ghoulie's not your regular zombie from a scary movie.
Unlike most zombies, which are hideous and furious.
Ghoulie was more on the lines of being lost, and curious.
He stared at the snowflakes, which shined like diamonds in the sea.
His stare seemed cold and blank, as if his mind was thought free.

Ghoulie held a snowflake, but it didn't melt in his hand.
There's something about him that you'll have to understand.
The one thing that was the most told:
Zombies, like Ghoulie, have hearts that were cold.
This poor child zombie, who looked and felt like a broken doll.
He actually didn't feel like he was broken; he didn't feel anything at all.
With his cold heart, Ghoulie's body could never be warm.
He was trapped in an empty, hollow, and rotten form.

Snow began to fall harder, like angry bees from a swarm.
A frightened villager was blinded by the snowstorm.
She didn't see Ghoulie, and crashed right into him.
Once she saw Ghoulie, it left her with a feeling of grim.

The frightened villager's name was **Kerry**.
Kerry screamed at Ghoulie, thinking he was scary.
Ghoulie growled at her, and yelled the word, "Brains!"
He stood tall, overtowering her, while showing his veins.
As Ghoulie's approach was coming near,
Kerry ran away, and dropped a photograph in fear.

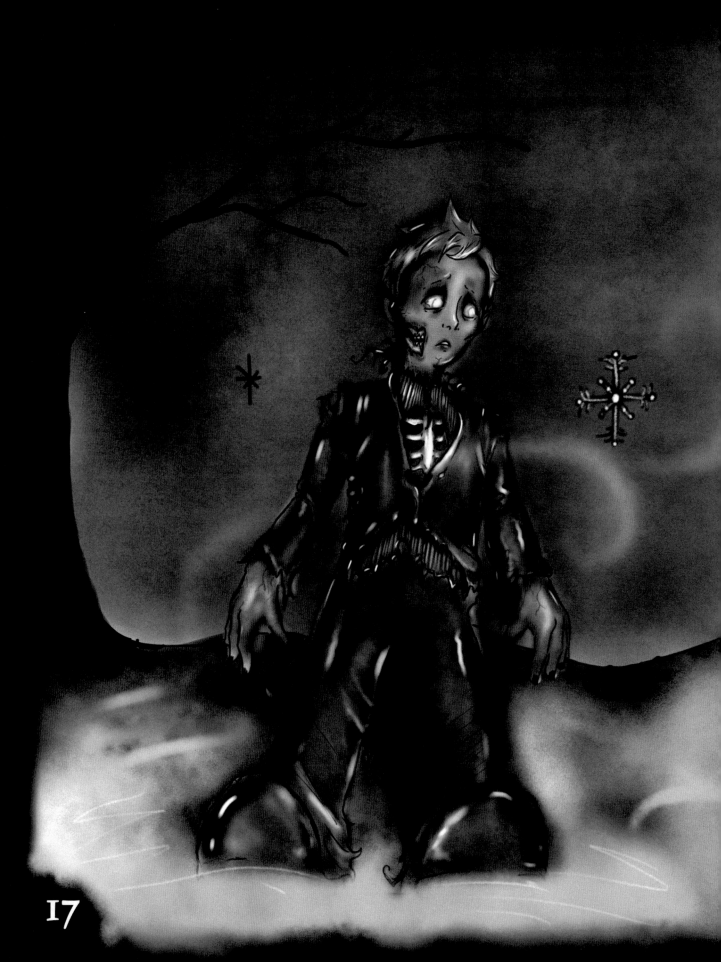

Ghoulie stopped his growling when he saw the photo.
Under the streetlight, the photo seemed like it began to glow.
It left Ghoulie with something that he did not know.
The snow-covered photograph was a picture of Kerry and her son.
They were decorating a Christmas tree, which seemed like a lot of fun.
Ghoulie stared at the picture for hours,
while ignoring the heavy snow showers.

The thing Ghoulie didn't know about Kerry's photo,
was that she waited on tables, so her income was low.
She only had enough to buy one picture at a time.
She kept it with her, to remind her when life was sublime.
Her son's name was Joseph, but she always called him **Joe**.
Due to a tragic car accident, she lost her son a long time ago.

As Ghoulie held the picture of Kerry and her boy,
he began to slowly remember a feeling, called *joy*.
Ghoulie even began to decorate a tree of his own.
He held the snowflake to the tree, and let out a joyous groan.

22

Ghoulie noticed that the snowflake in his hand had started to drip.
He watched the snowflake, while he curled his lip.
His eyes followed the drop of water, as if he was spellbound.
Then he saw his shadow, on the snow-covered ground.

Ghoulie began to chase his own shadow.
He even followed it through the frozen meadow.
Ghoulie, at this point, childishly started to believe,
his shadow was a person, who didn't want to leave.
The more time with his shadow, Ghoulie would spend.
He began to remember something, like having a *friend*.

25

Some of the townspeople were spying on Ghoulie.
They followed him, by hiding near some bushes and trees.

27

The townspeople were led by a man, called **Ted**.
Ted was one of the survivors from the attack of the living dead.
He saw Ghoulie, and it left him a terrible feeling of dread.
He told the other survivors, "It may look like a child, but don't be misled.
It could join the other zombies, and there will be more trouble ahead."

30

Ghoulie's shadow led him inside an old, dusty, and decayed farmhouse. The home at one point in time was owned by a farmer, and his spouse.

The interior of the farmhouse was nothing short of a catastrophe.
He stopped following his shadow, once he saw a painting of a family.

33

While Ghoulie walked toward the painting, he noticed a can of paint.
He dipped his fingers into the can, and fixed his biggest complaint.
As he placed his hand on the painting, he no longer felt discomfort.
He began to remember another important word, called *comfort*.

Angry townspeople rushed through the door.
Ted screamed at Ghoulie, with a powerful roar!
He marched at Ghoulie, holding a tree branch as a spear.
Ghoulie, at this point, began to feel something called *fear*.

38

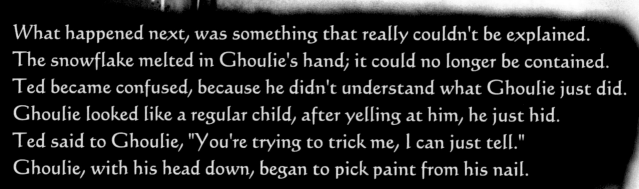

What happened next, was something that really couldn't be explained.
The snowflake melted in Ghoulie's hand; it could no longer be contained.
Ted became confused, because he didn't understand what Ghoulie just did.
Ghoulie looked like a regular child, after yelling at him, he just hid.
Ted said to Ghoulie, "You're trying to trick me, I can just tell."
Ghoulie, with his head down, began to pick paint from his nail.

The townspeople were surprised to see something they couldn't understand.
They saw that Ghoulie painted himself, with the family in the farmland.

Kerry yelled at the angry mob, " Stop! Leave him alone! You're scaring him!
He's not a creature from the dark, or something so grim."
Ted argued with Kerry, " That thing will be more dangerous in the long run."
Kerry replied to Ted's argument, " No! He's not dangerous, because he is my son."
Ghoulie was still afraid of the angry mob, so he hid in the darkness.
Kerry told everyone to leave, because he was harmless.

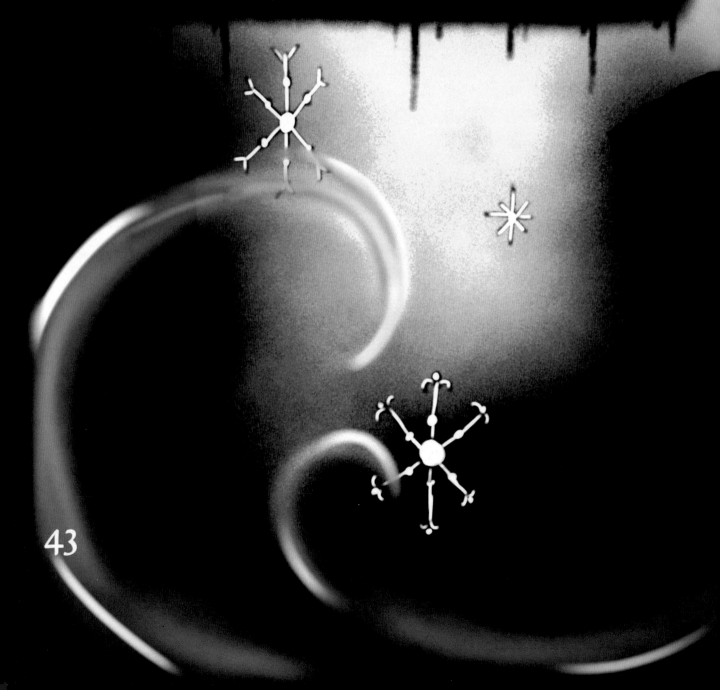

They all agreed to leave Ghoulie alone, and walked away.
Kerry was the only one who decided to stay.
She finally spoke to Ghoulie, " Joseph, can you come out from below?"
Ghoulie continued to hide in the darkness, while shaking his head no.
Kerry tried again, " It's me, your mother, do you hear me... Joe?"

46

Ghoulie slowly came out of hiding, and walked up to Kerry.
He gave her back the picture, with a look of wary.
Kerry no longer thought that he was scary.

Kerry's smile shined brightly.
She held her lost son, tightly.

Ghoulie, or in this case, Joe, learned something very clear.
Through joy, friendship, comfort, and even fear;
from the tiniest of creatures, to the great dark above.
Anyone can feel a special feeling, called *love*.

The End

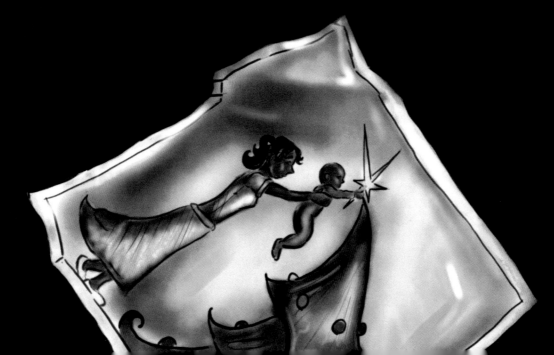